A Decade and A Half

In My Own Words: Poems & Prose

MAYA DANAE MANLEY

First Printing, 2017

ISBN 978-0-9985210-1-5

13th & Joan Publishing
500 N. Michigan Avenue, Suite #600
Chicago, IL 60611

www.13THANDJOAN.COM

*For my mother. Without you, A Decade and a
Half may have turned out differently.*

*For those I've met along the way, there is a
part of you that lives within the pages of this
book. Thank you.*

Contents

Introduction

This journey began after I sent a text to my mother. I'm sure it read "Mom I want to write a book." There was no plan, there were no ideas, no material to go into said book, but I wanted to do it. I had no idea that months later, I'd be in the process of publishing my own works. Writing has always been a hobby for me. It's something that I do in response to my life, or in response to the lives of others, or what's happening in the world. I started writing poetry in 8th grade. As an assignment, we were supposed to write a poem on a word. For some morbid reason, I still don't know, I chose the word "death". It's the first poem I can remember writing, and afterwards came "Story of a People" and maybe a hundred others. From there, writing was like a friend, something I could always do. It didn't require much of me, like a person would and despite the awful hand cramps and the graphite or ink smeared on my palm (because I'm left handed), I loved it. From that first interaction, came this. This is a collection of feelings about people and thoughts and things. Some of the content is likely thoughts that I was a little too afraid to say out loud, at the time.

Writing this book took a lot, especially the amount of emotion and rawness that I poured into it. There are bits and pieces of my family, my friends, and myself in here. But it's honest. And that's one thing that I can appreciate. I hope you do too.

Chapter 1:
Pain

"Turn your wounds into wisdom."
– Oprah Winfrey

There is No Way to Begin

There is no one way to begin.
It's hard to summarize.
Can't list the pain in those eyes.
Losses outnumber the wins.
And some question why the bad things
Burden good people.
In the frame of mind
Can barely feel.
Numb to even the echoing bass.
How tired the body seems
To charge but never get full.
Hungry for help, a savior, a
Moment of peace.
Hard isn't the word, too small to
Cover the atrocity or
Envelop the problem, never understood
Into the void.
Shouting.

Natural World

Unknown to each other,
    But bending, arcing, stitching together.
Rays of change cast spotlights on each scrap.
The tired roots seek one thing,
    The final piece;
    Scattered and stretched thin
    but strong.
It's hard to hold a grip.
Pits, craters collect together
    lonely, restless nights.
Nights on which the air was too cool
    for the season,
    and the dogs got to spend moments
    inside.
Nights that made bugs shrivel or loot or
    push to and fro.
Each marked by a star, a light, something
    permanent
    that could only fade
    with time.
Locked, tied, shut out like the blackest
    spot in the sky.
Where lovers had to be placed on shelves and
    in measured grooves.

Ruthlessly each is fogged, each interpretation
     of the matter its own.
Taking new hold in old soil
     wanting badly to return home.
A wave, a kiss, a stare goodbye,
     quietly marked with a concrete
     "x" and dirt dug up and turned
     over.

See, You've Forgotten Me Already

See you've forgotten me already.
You told me in a fit of pain that you were
Grateful.
That you were grateful I cared enough to love you,
to love you when you felt unlovable.
Grateful that I was unlovable too.
We could only fathom trouble and hurt.

So we built a house,
not at all tangible but real in every way.
And together we hid,
steering clear of reality.
It worked for a while,
Allowed us to stay away from turmoil,
from the things we couldn't handle.
I got stir crazy.
It seemed to me that hiding
wasn't the solution.

So I left you,
I left the house,
I left behind a little piece of me.

Wrapped with a bow
with a card that read,
"For you, something to remember me by."
I was hoping you would.
I was hoping you too would leave the house.
You'd board it up,
soak it in gas,
and light it up as you let go.
But take the piece of me with you.

I thought you would find me
as you found yourself.
You'd realize life isn't all bad,
I thought I was being an example,
you'd realize we could surpass anything.
And like the last piece of a jigsaw puzzle,
Complete the chapter.
I got my hopes up.

I OWE MY BODY APOLOGIES

Welts don't fade like memories
or sorries.
The whole of it battered
Resembling the hull of
A ship that's weathered
Too many storms.

Legs speckled, abstract
Paintings, summer nights
That dragged on too long
Into the brush of the dawn.

Arms riddled and
Slashed, much too hard
To hide. Conversation
Starters like tattoos I
Got on early
Mornings clouded with sangrias, maybe
something stronger.

Bruised and stretched
Thin with marks,
Few intentional
Blades dulled
No one's at
Fault.

Think of You Often

I recall having to remind you to call me
    As if you were someone's grandmother
Missing a few screws.
    Having to tell you what I wanted for my birthday
Because I was high maintenance and spoiled.
    Having to listen to your autobiography
On the nights we could only reminisce about
    The times we weren't struggling
Or too drunk on exhilaration to make good choices.

I think of you often
    Of the way your hands
    gripped the steering wheel during traffic.
Or the way your brows
    Pushed together.
Even the way you hummed along to
    Every song I blasted in my room when studying,
To show we could get through this.

I kept trying to replay these moments
    Especially when my mind was as still as waves.
When my mind triumphed even the fastest sprinter
    And climbed every height in its reach.

They are on loop like your favorite song.
    Overplayed in my head like terrible pop music.
Too loud to focus on,
    Too prevalent to ignore.

Millennials

category compiled
with ailments and
stigmas attached.
Misunderstandings
too frequent
hopes too high
so many of us alike
we tweet that we can't stand each other
and no one gets us
but someday when
we've built our own
it won't feel too heavy,
or look too gross
there won't be any puss,
no scabs.
Just promise me this,
don't be hard on the kids.

HER NUMBER

The digits were fresh in your mind.
I overheard her laugh at your terrible joke.
In my mind you were talking to me instead.

Foot

A foot away,
There's a foot of space between us,
Only separated by a foot of things unsaid.

It's a feeling like no other
Knowing there's nothing left to do.
The color drained itself
From your eyes, too tired to
Prop themselves open.

The whispers of the inevitable
Were evident
A lone tree were you
The rest of us clumped together
Like violets in the underbrush.
Braced for whatever.

Only separated by a foot of things unsaid.

An Out Loud Letter to You

And one day things changed / I started feeling like you knew. / You knew the chains that changed me / I started thinking you knew that all my problems were simple. / Without a doubt / that I seemed to stress myself out / and let the little things chew me up inside. / Outside you started acting like you cared / as if we shared the same fire / and you stoked that desire / to get over it all. / But the situation went haywire / eyelids seemed tired / brains unraveled their wires. / I started to reminisce / memorialize everything we'd experienced / it made no difference / nothing was the same. / I started feeling that our / connection / traveled to its end / and that I was without a friend. / And that those connecting flights / had reached their heights / and ultimately their plights. / So you started thinking that I wasn't / worthy enough. / And I / started thinking I wasn't worthy enough / as if worth had escaped me. / The God awful truth was that / friendship was the equivalent to / photo shop. / Easy to download and not update. / Our bands had popped

/ flinging us to opposite sides. / Me against you. / You in the corner and I, too. / Cries on the inside / built trenches on the outside / hearts on the left / burned bridges to the right. / And I started thinking / the mountains were high enough and / the valleys were low enough and / the river was more than wide enough / to keep me from getting to you. / I couldn't reach you. / And you didn't try to reach me. / One harsh reality. / Streams going down my face / formed rivers at your base / capital letters formed with haste / that covered my throat in a thick paste / and I yearned for a taste / of what we had again…/ what we found with each other / what we bound with each other. / And I started wondering / if you still thought about me / felt for me / acted for me / dreamed of me / wondered about me / changed because of me. / Do you still love me?

A Place for Me

To the ones I've loved before,
    Do you ever reminisce?

That's a rhetorical questions.
    I'm sure you don't,
    because I don't.
    I try not to.

It only leads
    only lead to a single thread.
    A piece threatening
    to break away.
    Threatening to bring the
    whole tapestry to shreds.

I can't figure out these scenarios
    in my head.
    Who kept everything together?
    And who didn't want to

I have the strange urge
    to place the blame on myself.
    It's easier this way.

So I guess I'm telling you
    to keep a place for me.

Faith

I can't remember the last time we talked before now. I didn't know you or how you'd been holding up. Truth is, I thought about you everyday for a month. If we're being honest I wished the worst on you. But on this day the "Good Christian" in me told you that whatever you were going through wasn't strong enough to defeat you. And the next day the "Good Christian" in me would check on you. You can't front, nothing's getting better. There's nothing you want to talk about because you don't want to cry or inconvenience me. You pushed against my push. Saying you couldn't explain it. That you were just tired of being down out. You couldn't do anything right. Couldn't find a reason to keep going. You didn't think you had a purpose and life was a lie. I told you to talk to God. You played the victim. But you were and I didn't understand the circumstances. I told you not to hang your head. So we didn't talk for a while. I wasn't helpful. You didn't want to hear me or anything I had to say. But you've always been like that, ever since middle school. Next time we spoke it was because I texted you. We made small talk until I got a little too deep, too far back in time. But you went with it. The way you always have. So we talked about the time we'd spent apart. I talked different. So did you. Before you derailed the train. Seems like you waited until I missed you to tell me. You were doing the things you used to. I told you not to explain. You know the stuff you were on before we met. Before I'd hope you'd be fine, but instead you'd become a stereotype. "Imma die someday," was your justification. But we'd had this conversation too many times for you not to get it: That you are loved and you are somebody's son. And somebody's brother. But I said my piece. Donated my two cents. I had so much faith in you. You had so much faith in me. But for different reasons.

"I can be changed by what happens to me.
But I refuse to be reduced by it."
- Maya Angelou

     A DECADE AND A HALF

Chapter 2: Power

"They are just beautiful souls learning to love themselves in an abyss that doesn't love them." - Maya Manley

For the Queens, with love

Baby girl with sparkles on your skin and
glitter in your hair
You were born for this
You were made to outdo and overcome.
Attractive to many, untouched by all.
Queen.

Natural Disasters

Only God can take from me what I know
    So you may blaze through, barrel through like
    hurricanes on the East coast.
Leave me among the shards of glass, plastic chairs, and
    dominoes.
Dispose my body like spoiled milk or wash me down
    the eye of a drain circled by tap water and bleach.
Because water levels rise and dust settles and synapses
    keep firing.
You can take me away from the very environment you
    gave me to fix
And bury me under whitewashed lies.
But what I know to be true is only mine to shout,
    scream, and spread.

To Whoever Needs Encouragement

Don't forget to breathe when you walk out there.
You'll take yourself out of the running quicker than
    your competition.
Push your shoulders back, flash those tic tac white
    teeth.
They won't get the best of you.
Save your superpowers for those who need them.
Be a witness to your success
So when they spit on your grave you turn them over
    till they're sick.

Woeman

take   on everything
                women.

                silver-haired and red-shod,
                in front of a packed house,

                        conference,
                World Summit.
                A professor,
                        The author
                                        is an
authority on   culture.
                        Response struck a

        note.
                        Recounting
    criticism   lobbed at her   not
of her   of her appearance.

Woeman (con't)

The (male)
wrote
she was less fit
for "The Undateables,"
            for the lovelorn disabled or disfig-
ured.
            Mutely accept
Ms.   with good cheer
                        wherever
            with
ugly   too brainy
      Clever Women.
  Time has not mellowed her take.
When you look at me on the telly   say
she should be
explained.

"Those that don't got it, can't show it.
Those that got it, can't hide it."
                    - Zora Neale Hurston

Chapter 3: Blackness

"Just because we're magic doesn't mean we're not real."
— Jesse Williams

STORY OF A PEOPLE

The catcalls from the supreme race –
Echoing in the back of my mind.
They speak of me and my brothers and sisters
as though we are not children of God.
They constantly remind us of those days we
were property.

Raised as Kings and Queens,
Raised to love ourselves...
Ripped from our roots and chastised
by strangers the generations following the originals
were raised to fear "them."

Too scared to shield ourselves from the deafening,
unkind we went without protest.

We were now a lost people without a voice.
We could not find a pathway to a better lifestyle.

Saved by a nation of kids.
They brought with them a power that aided our cause.
Made them think.
Together we skirmished through setbacks and mourned our losses.

And count the blessings that come along with his dream..

Unstoppable.

How Many Bullets?

Everyone knows you cannot hide the truth. But you can kill it. You can bury it alive with lies and courtroom opening statements and denial. The truth can so easily be denied. That's what's kept the shackles tight around gray, callused ankles. What's kept brains locked in treasure chests and no x's marking the spots. They've managed to write on paper how free we are but they're still dancing around us, chanting. A mantra they've written , scribbled on our foreheads, our wrists. Taped above our desks. "One nation, under God, indivisible, with liberty and justice for all."

We Are Sorry

We are all sorry.
We are sorry that you had to sit still pretending not to
be who you are.
We are sorry that the nuclear family ideal has diluted
and then destroyed the concept of kinship.
We are sorry we want to save the world by saving
ourselves first.
We are sorry that doctors use big, uncomfortable
words to choke ability.
We are sorry that parents use small, comfortable words
to stifle potential.
We are sorry we divided you into categories in order to
process you, to make sense of you.
We are sorry we watched your struggle turn into a
romantic comedy and tuned in to view it.
We are sorry we tried to reduce you to an essence,
because your aura was too hard to swallow, to
baroque to understand.
We are sorry that we can't accept why the world
revolves around the sun and not us.
And we are sorry that magic you contain will never
be useful because it's guarded by our systems and
relative values we're too lazy to reconstruct.
We are only sorry.

     A DECADE AND A HALF

The Color Black is Essential

"Black is the absence of color." The absence of color is merely an attempt to describe something in words that doesn't fit any label. Black is sweater that slims you down, tucks in your thighs. Black is "The Revolution Will Not Be Televised." Black is that eyeliner you so often flick and wing. Black is sweaty Saturdays on the blacktop with your boys and a ball. Black is how you like your dark roast Starbucks coffee. Black is paving roads without cement. Black is your perception of anything other than you. Black is as left behind as that last step you took. Black is that marbled composition book you fill with notes about Shakespeare, George Bush, and the Three-Fifths Compromise. Black is the curly, kinky, nappy, straight tresses that sprout from coconut nourished roots. Black is "don't venture there, it's too shady." And cross the street if he's darker than khaki. Black is whistling Vivaldi because it sounds just as good as the Jay-Z your homeboy blasts from his Impala. Black is profitable and case study. Black is fresh jays, temp fades, bundles, and dime bags. Black is sagging pants and penitentiary. Black is knowledge and power, style and art. Black is mahogany, mocha, caramel, Hershey, midnight, any genetic sequence you could think of. Black is as necessary as a left and right shoe but disappears like socks in a dryer. Black is anything that is worth something. Black is the new black.

On a Wednesday During Homecoming

*On A Wednesday During Homecoming,
Because We Took a Picture...*

I opened a squeaky pine door with a dark finish
to a room of writers and poets who expected
a typical day at the office. Eager to touch
pen to paper, to scribble an oath or proverb.
Outside of their refuge the real world sim-
mered. A friend shook and stomped, anger
and hurt boiling inside her. I hadn't realized
my own feelings were apart of this. Before
I managed to make it through a climb, steep
and tiring, flanked by stone pillars. But at the
peak there was no celebration for me making it
through the day, for me not speaking on my reli-
gion, or offending anyone. I made it through the
day I'll remember as the day I felt hate. I walked
through the single door. Into the single room where the
a/c switched in awkward intervals and the aluminum
system itself creaked with the weight of ghosts. Where
teenagers talked about teenage shit and phones buzzed
and emojis littered the screen. Life somehow continu-
ing. The mustard yellow, velvet couch laughed at me.
It knew my turmoil before it even boiled. But when it
finally did I spoke with my hands. Unpainted nails, not
shaped by files, flicked and waved. Expressing the words
I couldn't bring my southern self to utter in front of an

elder. A single voice raised and others faded. Eyes turned to search a body, my body. News articles and segments, slurs, documentaries, Trump supporters, history, MLK, flags, hashtags. All spilled over her lips, unspoken, like water being poured from a pitcher in the summertime. The lemons that floated in the solution shifting to the bottom, to be saved for a later time. They puddled at her feet. Around the ears of peers. Questions were fabricated from bystanders. I had not one answer. But the blood of those before multiplied. Filled my body. Red. Angry. The simple quote took out an infantry, a few special teams. The body operating only by the caffeine buzz. From the writer's room, to the checkered floor of Pressly backed by a poet who knew everything of my struggle but the feeling. I was quoted and my argument passed on to an overseer. Who knew nothing of my struggle or feeling, I managed to place a placid smile, a resting face for people to look at. For people to ignore. Before my cheek was placed on a mother's shoulder, not my own. And the sobbing began. The quiet sniffle, the periodic wiping, the gnarled lips bent to better amplify the shouts that still landed without a thud. Discarded. I was backed by a poet and a mother and a few teenagers. But I didn't return to the room for an hour. The mother and I walked the forest green campus to the bottom of the hill. On the look out for hell. Searching for a reset button. Anything. Down wide, brick corridors lined with shiny, etched metal, weighed by a heavy heart my vocal cords were stretched silent. Thin. I said nothing. I let the mother speak. Heard a few gasps materialize. Watched a couple smiles dwindle. Had my hand held. It was then, in the moment, where I knew what it meant to be hopeless. What it meant to be between a hard place and rock. I started my day with no intentions to end it in tears. I'd done nothing wrong…we'd done nothing wrong. Only had my faith in humanity decrease and my naivety escape. As ignorance is bliss it's not justifiable. As American flags are symbolic it's not a hall pass. As color is a trait it is not ammunition. We are not vandals.

Oct. 5, 2016 – 8:16 pm

CRISP WHITE NICE

Like air forces fresh out the box
Or frilly lace socks for your cream church shoes
Or the dress you were shrined in for your christening
and then your baptism.
Or the liberals you protest with.
Or the starched shirt for your first and last graduation.
Or the funeral service that you're the most essential to.

In Loving Memory of...

Sandra.
Tamir.
Eric.
Brandy Martell.
Kayla.
Kelly.
Jordan.
Anastacio.
Mario.
Mike.
Jonathan.
Meagan.
Guadalupe.

A EULOGY

We recognize the lives of those who are no longer
    with us and those who will go down fighting for
    something bigger than each of us combined
Here lies the lives of bodies riddled with scars or words
    and past worlds.
Simply put, here you king or queen.
Thank you
On behalf of generations to come
My sons and his sons and their sons.
You're appreciated.
Your efforts will not go unseen, unheard, or
    unreciprocated.
I'll end with this, if I'm half as brave as you, I may be
    something too.

"How do you pay homage to someone? You
say their names."
- Andrea Cohen

"I swear to the Lord I still can't see
why democracy means everybody but me."
- Langston Hughes

Chapter 4:
Here

"We must thank God not only for putting us in the right place but also for uprooting us out from wrong places."
– Jorge P. Guerrero

Gena Drive

I won't tell you about the dead tree, I've climbed many times before, sitting in the middle of the front yard. I won't tell you about the grand fence circling the neighbors, whose names I can never remember. I won't tell you about the cousins, aunts, uncles, that lived in the room atop the stairs or the many fish frys we've had together. I won't even mention the hundred pictures stuck to the refrigerator with magnets from as far as South Africa and Tokyo. The truth is I miss the Sundays spent in the living room. And the country ham searing on the stove. The coffee being made when I had an early morning workout and no one was ready to go. My grandparents smiling, my little brother, too. I can't stop thinking about my little sister, getting bigger and bigger. She probably doesn't even know my name. I miss the snapshot 70s, powder pink bathroom. The mute smell of tobacco from your ashtray, or the newspaper clippings littering the dining room table. I miss seeing you on a daily basis. I don't get the same luxuries as other little girls. Because the dead tree wasn't dead until after you left. The grand fence wasn't rusted until you left. I can't even tell you the last time I went to a fish fry. All those things stopped when you disappeared. I don't know why. But it seemed life as we knew it no longer wanted to be

known. It had only been photographed, the way annoy-
ing parents do at all your big events, graduations, birth-
days, you know. Yet life had changed. The photographs
don't mean much to me now. They only remind me of
the things I used to have.

In Green

Pistols flared setting off runners.
Shouts echoed cheering on players.
Voices whispered stringing together secrets.

The grass and the 'wildcats' and the trees
meld together.
A big bowl of forest green.
The American flag floats
in the vigorous wind.

Footsteps got etched into the dirt,
into the bleachers, into the trail.
A sense of camaraderie blanketed us.
The visitors, the regulars, the die hards.

Pristine skies, fields,
bases, corner arcs
all in line.

The order didn't feel stark.
The disarray didn't feel chaotic.
Every person had a piece.
Every piece had a place.
Every place had a purpose.

GEORGIA: POOR & PLAYERS

1. Get deep in the city and find a gold mine or a blood bath.
2. Drive far from terminus and see how far you get before your heart grows or aches.

23. Plant a tree where you stake your home, declare it's yours, when the roots catch drive a knife into the bark.

25. everywhere you go take an appetite or a gun.

For the Last Time

Take a piece off the side table planted by the door
Like you would've with the car keys or a bag of
     cheerios
Pocket it.

Take a picture of the scrawly, chicken scratch
     handwriting littered on the corner baseboard of the
     office.

Take a walk through with your memories clutched in
     your hand, they'll drip, slip through the slivers of
     your fingers.
The same way they will from your memory.
Count the notches on the kitchen door frame
     documenting every family member's height and
     make it your passcode.
Smash that clock that ticked too loudly at night during
     your heroic attempts to get through a scary movie
     alone
Or pack it up and take it with you.
Take the Nativity statue from the mantel, too.
It'll be like the Ouija board you'll later wish for.

Lock the attic and pray one more time that the
neighborhood kids won't bother you for water.
And on your way out pull the screen door tight and
try not to let the cool air out.

"Freeing yourself was one thing; claiming
ownership of that freed self was another."
- Toni Morrison

Chapter 5: Smile & Pain II

"If you want to be happy, be."
— Leo Tolstoy

I have watched my parents. Seen them give each other small knowing looks. I witnessed them dance in the dying grass and an autumn breeze that seemed to whisk them into a different world. I've watched the kitchen turn into their own private island. I'm sure there was a time when I knew they couldn't be without each other. They spent a many a nights out, me with my grandparents, naive to how anyone could love like that. Pendergrass wasn't their medicine, their remedy; they took smaller doses of Vandross. Dad used to hold my mother close as if he was scared if he let her go she'd never return. But she would. She loved him. They used to dance, every blue moon, and the stereo would blast eighties love songs from the office. And I used to sit right next to speaker; immune to the bass. He looked at her sometimes with glassy eyes, and I couldn't tell what the problem was, but she could. My skin riddles with goose bumps when I recall these things.

As a kid, there was no heat. Part of me knew it was there. However, I was a kid. I still am, but that doesn't mean that you can't feel the heat. The hotness and intensity of what they had is present in my memories, and I've felt it myself. The heat of it is the most tangible shred of their love that I have left. All I have to hold on now. I was the sunrise they crafted. The starry sky they gazed at. But it all spilt in two. The sky almost blue flickered before shifting to a cold black. They're divorced now.

An Ode to the Sister Living in the Frame

I've owned you for over a decade now.
A frame, still sits on my dresser,
tickled pink.
There's a bow on its middle
a wonderful picture under.
Two carefree daughters
learning how to be sisters.

You matched the second bedroom
I lived in.
There were tender pink dots,
sprawled haphazardly on you.
There's nothing else attached to your body
only memories in their most material form.

I was six years old,
it was getting cold out,
no one could drive a wedge between us.
I haven't seen you in six, almost seven, years.

But I remember the scent of the Aquaphor
you spread religiously on your lips,
the short, shoulder length braids anchored by beads,
the terrible pop song by Clique 5
that made me want love.

Something I knew nothing about then,
and pieces of now.
I don't know what college you're going to,
or even your boyfriend's name.
But I know your heart because,
it's etched into the frame.

Pecan Beauty

Eggs. five.
Pecans. three cups.
Baking powder. A teaspoon.
I know that recipe like a prayer.

The canola oil popped
   in the pan.
It singed my bare feet.
Pour the mix in the shell.
Put pecans on the top
Around the edges of the shell

The pie was just as pretty
   as her.
The butter just as smooth
   as her skin.
The lumps of the crushed pecans
   just like the coils of black hair
   placed like a crown on her head.
It made me feel at home.
The spoon covered with thick Karo syrup
   like the toothbrush loaded with gel
   that somehow tamed my curls.

She was a fierce as the canola oil.
As southern as the pecans.
As together as the mixture.
As beautiful as the caramelization.

NEVER KNOWN A BOY LIKE YOU

Never known a boy like you
Black with broad shoulders
And flashy white teeth
Deep cuts in your chocolate cheeks
And baby hairs dotting your hair line.
You talk with a southern educated drawl
That somehow manages to cross all your ts.
You walk with purpose one slew footed step after next.
Somehow always managing to call the most positive
attention to yourself.
It's a wonder how someone like you pays attention to me.

Eloquent

Words seemed to string
Themselves together
Managed by your
Tongue
Orchestrated calmly,
With ease.
Defying what it meant to
Speak.
What it meant
To persuade me
To submit.
Calling and crashing
Waves that soothed
Even the sharpest mind.
Baiting her, even
Him, luring, and
Casting.
I watched amused.
Immune to the tones,
Astonished at your presence.

An Apology

I asked you years ago that I wanted an
apology. Or I wanted to. I wanted an
apology because you owed it to me. You
never said "I'm sorry" to my face. As if a different place pushed all your problems to go
away. They didn't, they wouldn't hide. As
much as you ignored my voice, no amount
of closure could consume you. I wanted
approval. That somehow, someway I was
doing just fine. I couldn't coax that out of
you. Nothing could coax anything out of you.
I wanted validation. Despite what anyone
said or felt. Despite what I'd been through.
You took that from me, the type of love only
a father can give a daughter. You stripped from
my hands and buried them deep in sand. There
was nothing left for me to hold onto. I have pictures of you, but I don't know you. And as much
as you like to say you know me…you don't

Maya Manley – May 17, 2015

JIM

Sometimes when you answer the phone
I know you're busy.
Other times I know you're minutes away
from falling asleep.
And then there are times
when your energy radiates.
Like when a mother
starts yelling at a child over the phone
and you can imagine the spit flicking off her lips.

I'll tell you to perk up, buttercup.
And you often tell me to just be happy.
I didn't know it was that easy.
Because when you're down,
I thought, nothing is easy.
Somehow, you make it just that simple.

It could always be worse
you say.
And I know,
but no one has seen the things you have
or counted near as many stitches.

So when it gets bad
I'll call you and you feel free to call me.

Everything has an answer with you.
This is my appreciation for that.
I wrote this for you.

God's Will

My grandmother called me last night. I remember the conversation vividly. Not because it happened yesterday but because of what she said. There's an old gospel song, kind of a hymn, but not really. The words say, "thank the grandmothers who are always praying," or something like that. She told me about my friends in my old neighborhood. How some were beginning to move away. The three seniors that we were all so proud of. My grandmother said the whole neighborhood's relying on me, to make Lovejoy something to be proud of. But back to the song, she heard it on the radio while going to church. It's her favorite song. She said she got so excited that the people next to her at the light probably thought she was crazy. I laughed at her honesty. She then told me why the song meant so much to her. 2 years ago, I'd just turned 14. I let the neighborhood down. So they sent me to Riverwoods. Where I met Hayley, Kaylin, Teraesa, Keon and Rodney. They lumped us into a classroom, wanted us to work on our behavior. I didn't go to school for two months. I'm not sure how I made it past eighth grade. I'm not trying to be funny but I think it was God's will.

I heard you Laugh Yesterday...

I heard you laugh yesterday. I had soccer practice in an hour and you lived near the field, so we stopped by, momma and me. You came to the door with rollers strategically organized on your head and covered with bonnet. You wore a blue house dress and black slippers. The minute you saw us, you launched into a story. We lingered in the hallway listening. Before lilting down the hallway, you with a mysterious limp. Your voice was doing the normal quiver. We sat on the brown leather sectional. Me near Paw Paw's assigned seat, Mom in a matching recliner, and you next to the chaise. "You see how swollen my foot is?" I relocated to the ground, opening the chicken noodle soup I'd gotten from the Dwarf House on Tara Boulevard. "How'd you manage to do that?" "I stepped up and missed." "How do you step up and miss?" "Talking and laughing with your father." "Where is he? Holler up there and get him." I was a third of the way done with my soup when I heard Paw Paw's stairlift creak with his weight and groan mechanically as he descended. You had gotten up to call him down which I told you I could've done. And he stepped clumsily into the kitchen, clearly off balance. My mother sat prying open boiled peanuts from the fruit stand down the street.

He took the steps one at a time before stopping by my mother, "Hey daughter." He smiled. I love that smile. He walked over to me and I kissed his cheek after he sat down. My grandmother asked how he slept after dialysis, I noticed the red stain on the gauze taped carefully to his arm. "Just fine Mary." MSNBC purred faintly in the background, there was another headline about Donald Trump and his attack on the Khans. You shook your head and laughed about a cartoon you saw in the paper about him. "And he was so orange, and his toupee was leaning off his head, and he looked so foolish." We laughed at your enthusiasm. Typical of you. I walked outside to grab the mail and picked up a couple of ice cream wrappers, the truck must've just left. There were some children riding bikes a tad too big for them down the tall hill behind me and the older boys of the neighborhood, some of whom I'd known since I was a little girl, were playing basketball. They were about to start their senior year of high school on the eighth and were ready to move to the city, Lovejoy could no longer contain them. I told them I'd see them later, the way I usually did when I came to visit. "You stopped to talk to those boys, huh?" Paw Paw asked. I couldn't help but laugh as I sat down to finish my soup. You asked me was I ready for school and did I help my mother out at home. I answered yes, like have a million times before. Then you asked my mom was I helping her out at home or ready for school, she answered no, like she had a million times before. I threw away my mom's trash along with mine and while I was up you asked for ice cream. The same Blue Bell, vanilla ice cream you'd been buying for decades. I brought the whole tub out and we sat together taking huge spoonfuls that froze our lips every time. My mom laughed at my granddad's antics after showing him a video of my baby cousin having his first lemon. He smiled that same smile again.

NOTHING I WANT

My grandma told me in a city almost shrined in gold, "They
ain't got nothing I want."
I thought she was trying to be brave.
I didn't know how true she was.
Ain't nothing you got worth my love or soul or time.
We work for what we want.

For Momma, with Sugar

I haven't forgot about you
You're on my mind like white on rice
Or corn on cobs.
Your southern rations keep me alive out here
In the land that ain't milk and honey.
I haven't been freed yet.
There's nothing like being a caged bird in a world with
    no Maya Angelou to hear my song.
But your love and God's love surround me.
So I imagine I'll be fine.

For my Best Friend

Saturdays are our thing. Black benches and sunbeams are our thing. Laughing at 2 a.m. when only procrastinating college kids and junkies are awake is our thing. Smiling, just because we were in the same place is our thing. One doesn't know love if it knocked them on their behind and stared into its eyes. But I do. Because doing our thing on any regular, dry heat, cloudless day is love. I smile when you laugh, and laugh till I cry, and cry until I can laugh again.

Burning fall leaves and the strong stench of Skoal tobacco etched into the memories that surround my mind. The remnants of books and old bills I used to draw on. Pictures lost under beds and remembered every Christmas. Shopping sprees just because and Wal-Mart runs when I wanted something new. My obsession with McDonald's, no Wendy's, I'm pretty sure it's Zaxby's. The time you called some lady a "yahoo" at an intersection.

And it's love. Love for you and love that continues to brighten day after day. Love that's strong enough to make you forgive and forgive because I haven't been the best I could be. Love. Love that's stitched into every memory. Because I say I hate that girl and you laugh at me. "You say that all the time but you'll be talking to her tomorrow, I know it." Or every time I slyly tried to ask for money and you gave it up even though you didn't have it to give. Love when you and I walked back and forth outside Murphy's on Mother's Day, arm locked in arm, because you wanted to enjoy the fresh air. Love when we sat in a car for hours just listening to jazz. The time you were my date to a wedding and it was just the two of us.

Love, for you and for me and love that touches everyone around us. Love the kids on the street wish they could have and love that sometimes reaches far beyond Orion. Love that only a best friend can offer to another. Love that surrounds us in envelopes of blankets and pine needles, even pecans. Love only you and I truly understand. And I love you, I love you, I love you because the things I couldn't give myself you offered to me willingly and nothing could ever replace that carved canyon in my heart that's been dug by you. But when you're gone I'll sit in the dust of that ditch and run my hands through the sand and string together a dusty castle that won't last forever but builds up the memories of us.

About the Author

Maya Manley is currently a sophomore at The Westminster Schools of Atlanta. She plays soccer for Concorde Fire and loves the game. She also enjoys reading, writing, and watching comedy specials. She has recently become more engaged in current events and human rights and hopes to pursue a  career in science, particularly in medicine. Maya plans to continue her writing journey in the years to come